DISNEY'S
WINNIE THE POOH'S
EASTER

BY BRUCE TALKINGTON

ILLUSTRATED BY BILL LANGLEY and DIANA WAKEMAN

DISNEY
PRESS

NEW YORK

FIRST EDITION
1   3   5   7   9   10   8   6   4   2

Library of Congress Catalog Card Number: 92-53441
ISBN: 1-56282-377-9

WINNIE THE POOH'S
EASTER

Winnie the Pooh felt a stirring to see the Hundred-Acre Wood in all its new spring finery. The magic of the season was shaking off the sleep of winter and opening up to all things new and wonderful, so Pooh was climbing the path that led to a very special place called "Up There," because that was exactly where it was, atop the highest hill in the forest.

He was enjoying himself thoroughly, and as a playful breeze whistled in one ear and out the other, he laughed out loud and cried, "No fair tickling!"

His laugh, however, ceased abruptly as his mouth opened around a very surprised "Oh."

It was the sort of "Oh" that popped out whenever Pooh wanted to say, "That's the most wonderful thing I've ever seen."

For in the middle of the clearing Up There, perched on its large end, pointing its small tapered nose up to the smiling sunlight, sat the biggest egg Pooh had ever seen! Shading his eyes, he stretched himself up onto the very tips of his toes until he lost his balance and suddenly found himself sitting down with a loud *thump!*

"My," thought Pooh as he rubbed the part of himself that had thumped the loudest, "that egg is as tall as Christopher Robin. Perhaps taller!"

The idea of an egg taller than Christopher Robin was quite enough in and of itself to keep Pooh puzzling for a very long time. Its size, however, wasn't the most surprising thing about the egg. It was all violet stripes and bright green squiggles, yellow polka dots and pink swirls!

After Pooh had thought about it a moment (quite long enough as far as he was concerned), he discovered that the egg made him want to laugh out loud. He had absolutely no idea why that should be, but there it was! What he did know, however, was that laughing out loud was not something one did all by oneself.

[2]

In a surprisingly short time, considering it was Pooh who was doing the fetching, the top of the hill was bustling with all of Pooh's very good friends.

"Oh my goodness," squeaked an amazed Piglet. "That is the most *un*-very-small egg I have ever seen!"

Gopher squinted and, holding up his thumb, surveyed the egg carefully. "If someone wanted to make breakfast out of this baby, they'd have to blast for sure!"

"This is nothin'," chuckled Tigger, bouncing back on his springy tail. "But I'll bet the look on the chicken's face was something to see! Hoo-hoo-*hoo!*"

"Oh, don't be so silly," snapped Rabbit. "It's obvious this egg has nothing to do with chickens or breakfasts!"

"Obvious to whom?" rumbled Eeyore. "If you don't mind my asking."

"You mean to tell me none of you knows what sort of egg this is?" demanded Rabbit.

"Well," hooted Owl, shifting his feet on his perch atop the egg, "it's *not* an owl egg. I can say that with certainty and not a small amount of relief."

"It's an Easter egg!" Rabbit announced triumphantly.

There was silence as everyone digested this revelation.

"Aren't we sort of too far west for *east*-er eggs?" Tigger finally asked, not because he knew what he was talking about, but because the quiet was making him restless.

"No, no, no!" moaned Rabbit. "Easter is a holiday, and it's now! This is the time of year everyone gives decorated eggs to one another. I have it on very good authority from my distant cousin, who is a personal acquaintance of someone who knows the Easter Bunny's gardener!" he added smugly.

"Ah!" replied Pooh. He'd found that pretending a thing was understood was sometimes very close to actually understanding it. Then it could be easily forgotten with no one the wiser...especially not Pooh.

"Why," muttered Eeyore, giving his tail a shake before sitting down, "would anyone do a thing like that?"

"Well," Rabbit answered somewhat hesitantly, "that is a little harder to explain." He paused. "It seems, at least from what I've been told, that these are very special eggs."

"Very special *how*, Bunny Boy?" Tigger wanted to know. "Don't keep us suspended. Out with it."

"It appears," Rabbit said slowly, "that they can talk."

"Ah!" Pooh said again, a little louder.

"To be specific," Rabbit sniffed importantly, "they are supposed to say how very much we care for one another."

They all looked at the egg for a very long time, with new respect.

"Hmph," said Gopher, breaking the silence. "I'll bet this egg says it *loud*!"

They all gathered close around the egg and listened carefully.

[10]

"It's not saying anything now," said Tigger in a disappointed whisper.

"P-perhaps it's shy," suggested Piglet.

"We haven't exactly been properly introduced," responded Eeyore. "Not that anyone has ever been in a hurry to introduce me."

"And eggs, no matter how large, can't have been around long enough to know how to make friends quickly," Owl reminded everyone.

"I imagine," said Piglet, giving the egg a gentle pat, "that it feels quite out of place."

"Perhaps if we make it feel at home, it'll feel more like talking," Pooh cried.

"But how does one make an egg feel at home?" asked Rabbit in exasperation.

Pooh smiled. "I believe I have an idea."

It seemed as if no time had passed at all before Pooh's plan was put into effect, and there on the highest hill in the Hundred-Acre Wood it suddenly appeared as if the giant egg were no longer the only Easter egg Up There.

Pooh had painted himself a bubbly pink with baby blue freckles. Tigger had acquired a checkerboard pattern of pastels.

Piglet resembled a very small, very red apple, while Owl was a sky blue color with a trim of fleecy white clouds. Gopher was the color of a ripe banana, and Eeyore was decked out in lavender polka dots.

"It has to speak sooner or later, doesn't it?" sighed Pooh after quite some time had passed. "I mean, if it's going to say it cares and all?"

[15]

"Maybe we have to tell it how much we care first," suggested Eeyore. "You know, just to break the ice?"

"How do we do that?" asked Piglet.

"The only proper way to speak to an egg," Owl informed anyone who cared to listen, "is when you are sitting on it."

"Maybe so," agreed Gopher, "but it seems to me that not just any whippersnapper who happens along can sit on an Easter egg. Doesn't seem to fit the blueprint somehow."

"I can tell you one thing for certain," said Tigger. "I wouldn't want anyone sitting on me unless I was pretty sure he knew what he was doing!"

Everyone began rubbing their chins and scratching their heads, furiously trying to figure out what they were going to do. One by one, they all turned to stare at Winnie the Pooh. Who in the Hundred-Acre Wood knew more about sitting than Winnie the Pooh did? Broad smiles spread slowly over their faces. "Oh yes!" they said to one another, and nodded. "Of course."

Pooh nodded and smiled along with them even though he had no idea what they were nodding and smiling about. It seemed the friendly thing to do.

Rabbit put his arm around Pooh's shoulders. "This time *I* have a plan, Pooh Bear."

"Ah!" said Pooh.

The next thing Pooh knew, Tigger was standing on top of the egg, tugging on Pooh's hands, while Rabbit stood beneath and pushed for all he was worth. Piglet and Gopher ran around in helpless circles, shouting advice as the egg began to sway erratically back and forth. Owl hovered above the activity and made disapproving comments regarding animals without wings.

But before anyone could get Pooh seated, let alone ask the egg anything, away it went, rolling down the hill, bright colors shifting like a pinwheel!

They chased the rolling egg downhill and up...

...through rushing streams and muddy spaces...

...across wide meadows...

...under bridges...

...and over valleys until...

...the egg rolled to a halt, spinning around on its side like a wayward bottle, turning more and more slowly until finally it stopped...with its tip pointing directly at Christopher Robin!

"What are you doing with my Easter egg?" he wanted to know.

"Delivering it?" Pooh suggested with a smile.

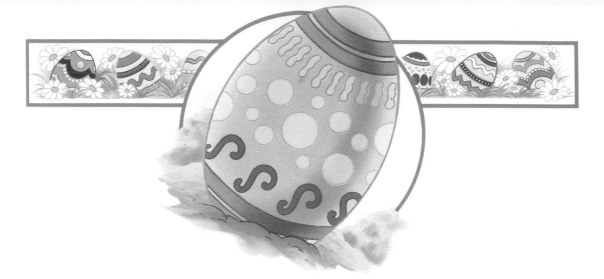

"Well," said Christopher Robin, looking over his decorated friends with a smile, "you certainly are dressed for the job!"

Tigger put his ear to the egg and gave a disgusted snort. "It's still not saying anything to anybody."

"Hmmm. Are you sure this is your egg, Christopher Robin?" asked Pooh.

"Actually, no," he admitted. "It's yours. All of yours. It was going to be a present from me, so I hid it in what I thought was a lonely place." He laughed. "It seems you beat me to my own surprise!"

"So when's it going to tell us how much it cares?" Eeyore demanded. "I mean, if that's what it's supposed to do."

Christopher Robin put his finger to his lips. "You just have to know how to listen. Watch."

Christopher Robin grasped the huge egg with both arms around its middle and began to twist the top. The egg slowly began to unscrew!

In a moment, Christopher Robin removed the top half of the egg and lifted out another egg painted to look very much like Winnie the Pooh!

"Oh my!" breathed Pooh.

"You haven't seen anything yet," laughed Christopher Robin, and he began unscrewing the Pooh egg.

One after another, each a bit smaller than the last, an egg in the image of each of Christopher Robin's friends was revealed.

The last, of course, was Piglet. It was a very small egg, but the delighted Piglet was used to very good things in very small packages.

"I'm going to keep mine next to my bedside table," decided Pooh after a long bout of thinking.

"Isn't that a strange place for an Easter egg?" asked Christopher Robin.

[26]

"Oh my goodness, not at all," chuckled Pooh. "Then the last thing it tells me before I fall asleep at night and the first thing it says when I open my eyes in the morning will be how very much somebody cares."

Christopher Robin put his arm around Pooh Bear's shoulders and scratched him behind an ear. "Happy Easter, silly old bear!"